# Our Farm

Diane E. Stango

Rosen
REAL
READERS

The Rosen Publishing Group, Inc.
New York

1

We live on a farm.

We see apples on our farm.

We see pumpkins on our farm.

We see a cow on our farm.

We see chickens on our farm.

We see a tractor on our farm.

# Words to Know

apples

chickens

cow

pumpkins

tractor